BILLIONAII
NIG
BY
VENUS RAY &
STACY-DEANNE

Stacy-Deanne

BOOKS FOR YOUR SOUL

Readers: Thanks so much for choosing my book! I would be very appreciative if you would leave reviews when you are done. Much love!

Email: stacydeanne1@aol.com
Website: Stacy's Website [1]
Facebook: Stacy's Facebook Profile[2]
Twitter: Stacy's Twitter[3]

To receive book announcements subscribe to Stacy's mailing

list: Mailing List[4]

Want recommendations on great BWWM books and authors? Stop by BWWM Books on Facebook and find some great reads!
BWWM Books[5]

---

1.   https://www.stacy-deanne.com/

2.   https://www.facebook.com/stacy.deanne.5

3.   https://twitter.com/stacydeanne

4.   http://eepurl.com/dFGzTL

5.   https://www.facebook.com/groups/936516153033358/

More Steamy Titles By Stacy-Deanne:

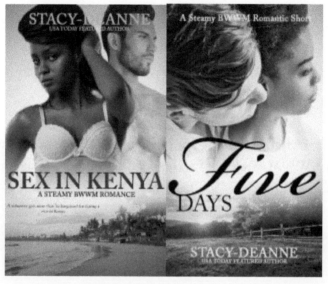

CHECK OUT THESE BOOKS and more at the link below. These titles are currently free in Kindle Unlimited!

http://amzn.to/2BSu1tf

CHAPTER ONE

At 36, James Kris was every woman's fantasy. Rich beyond belief, heart-stopping gorgeous, and enough style to put Gucci out of business.

The expensive clothes and fantastic haircut. The sculpted physique thanks to a personal trainer five days a week. His Instagram profile was something out of a movie.

What followed was a legion of thirsty women trying to get on his arm. Twenty-five-year-old Kelly Banks had worked for him for four years and seen dozens of bimbos try to worm their way into James' life. Their tactics made Kelly gag from laughing so hard. One even tried to convince James he'd gotten her pregnant, even though they'd never slept together.

As his assistant, Kelly had firsthand knowledge of what James did in his personal life and with whom.

Being the hottest eligible bachelor in town might have meant that he was a playboy. But he was so focused on his work that he barely went out. Dating was non-existent. All of this just made him hotter in her eyes. From the first couple of weeks of working with him, she got a crush, and before she knew it, she'd fallen in love.

Until James, she'd never even thought of being with a white man, let alone her boss. She wasn't against the idea, it's just that where she came from, the teeny, little, backwards black town of Caesar, Georgia, hell, there had been no white boys for her to date.

Once she moved to Atlanta, all that changed and she opened her heart to endless possibilities.

Many in Atlanta dated according to their status. Kelly's two best girlfriends did. Shana and Fay had both graduated from HBCUs with honors, had corporate careers, and of course were members of prestigious sororities. A man better not even look at them if he didn't have a degree.

Shana was so pitiful that a man not only has to have a degree, but one of a certain caliber just to get her number.

Kelly understood wanting to be with someone who could bring something to the table, but love should be more important. Who cared how many degrees someone had if the person didn't set your heart on fire or didn't make your skin melt when they touched you?

She loved Fay and Shana, but them heifers would be alone for the rest of their lives if they didn't ditch their snobbery.

As for James, he had no clue of how desperately Kelly lusted for him. How she dreamed of him every night and woke up soaking wet between her thighs afterwards. Despite how hard it had become, Kelly stayed professional and kept her libido under wraps at work. She did her best not to look at him too long or say something that he'd take as flirtation. Yet, they spent so much time together and sometimes it was hard to keep her desire for James at bay.

Other women didn't have the same problem.

However, now and then James would ask Kelly to do something that would normally be above and beyond what an assistant should do.

After James called her into his office the evening before his big charity auction, she knew it might be one of those times.

He rocked in the squeaky leather chair behind his shiny, black desk. "So there's one thing I need you to do for me, and it's going to sound weird."

She sighed. "You want me to pretend to be your wife again because some chick is bothering you?"

He laughed. "Not exactly."

"What?" She shrugged, her jet-black Brazilian waves draping across her shoulders.

"I want you to bid on me."

"Ah, yes." Kelly clasped her chestnut-brown hands, grinning. "The auction."

He swallowed, those angular cheeks flexing. "You know it's tonight?"

"Of course. You've been talking about it for weeks, plus it's been all over local media. Can I be honest, James?"

His sky-blue eyes sparkled. "You can be anything you *like*."

See, it was times like these that confused the hell out of her. He was always flirting, but he did it so subtly. Perhaps he didn't want a sexual harassment suit slapped on his ass, but now and then the tone of his voice grew deeper and his gaze always fell to her cleavage a few times during every conversation.

"Kelly?"

"Huh?" She shook from her thoughts. "Oh, sorry. What?"

"You wanted to say something?"

"Oh, yeah. This auction thing just seems immoral. Sorry, but in case you haven't noticed, I'm not too fond of human auctions. I don't know, maybe it's because of my ancestors being sold and bought like cattle."

He snickered. "It's not like that."

"But aren't you already being chased by every woman in Georgia? Hell,

every woman around the country? Why do you need to do this?"

"The Cancer Foundation is one of our company's biggest partners, and this is for a good cause."

She crossed her arms. "And its good publicity for you meaning for the company as well."

He shrugged in his crisp Armani shirt. "Will you bid on me?"

Kelly laughed. "What makes you think I got money to spend at an auction?"

His arched yellow eyebrows dipped. "This is for charity so the bids start low enough for anyone to participate. I believe the minimum bet is forty dollars." He raised an eyebrow, grinning. "What do you say?"

A thought flashed into her head that maybe this was his way of trying to get a date with her on the sly. But seeing how

James had more confidence than anyone she'd ever known, it seemed implausible that he wouldn't just ask her out.

"What will this be like?" She groaned.

"There's going to be a bunch of women bidding on the city's most eligible, rich bachelors. Whoever wins, gets a date with the guy of her choice for a night. That's it. It's harmless."

Kelly smirked.

His face dropped. "Cecilia Martinez's gonna be there."

"Your stalker?" Kelly joked, stroking her hair. "Gotta give it to her, she's persistent. She's been chasing you for years."

"I'd put a restraining order on her ass if her father wasn't the district attorney." He rolled his eyes. "Anyway, you know she's going to bid her entire bank account on me if she can. I'd rather have my dick run over than to go out with her. I can't stand her." He shuddered. "That little whiny voice and she's about five hundred pounds!"

Kelly scoffed. "James."

"And she sweats so much. I will *pay* you to outbid her." James' face relaxed. "Whatever you bid, I'll take care of it. Just don't let me go with Cecilia."

"Can't you ask someone else to do this?"

"Are you kidding?" He grimaced with a hairless face as smooth as a baby's bottom. "Nobody's gonna outbid her because they think she'll have her father arrest them or something."

Kelly laughed. "She can't do that."

"I put nothing past Cecilia. But yeah, she's already put out warnings to other women. You gotta help me, Kelly. I can't *stand* her." He gripped the desk, shaking his head. "Bid whatever you want. I can afford it. Just don't let Cecilia get me."

"Isn't this cheating?"

"I don't give a damn." The dimple in his chin moved in and out. "Just keep that sweaty bitch away from me."

"I don't know, James."

"Kelly, please. You'll be helping me and the cancer patients." He made a puppy-dog face. "Please?"

He didn't have to beg. Again, she didn't like the auction thing, but if she said no to going out with James, she'd never forgive herself. This could be her only chance to get close to the man of her dreams outside of their work relationship.

And who knows?

She caught his stare and his eyes flashed.

Maybe he felt the same way about her as she did about him.

Maybe.

"Okay." She nonchalantly shrugged. "I'll do it. But I don't have anything in my closet for a big-time charity auction."

"Really?" His sexy features twisted with mockery. "With all those outfits I bought you to accompany me places? Got them flown in from as far as Paris."

"Yeah, but this is high society and you know as well as anyone a woman can't wear the same dress twice." She sashayed closer to the desk. "If you want me to play the part then pay for me to play it."

He puckered his lips into a frisky smile. "Women will do anything to get a new outfit. Okay." He looked around, tapping the desk. "Hold on." He got his phone and Kelly perked up as he called Atlanta's most popular boutique, which catered to the local sports teams, film, and TV studios. "Yeah, and put it on my tab," he said into the phone. "Okay, Manuel. Bye-bye." James hung up the phone. "Done. Just go home and a beautiful dress that will make you the envy of the crowd will be there in a few hours."

She pulled one of her wavy strands. "What about my hair and makeup?"

"It looks great the way it is and you don't even need makeup."

"I'm not going to this event with celebrities and TV cameras unless I get a new hairstyle." She winked. "You feel me?"

He groaned. "You're something else, Kelly." He got on the phone again, this time calling one of Atlanta's most revered hair stylists who'd worked with two of the juiciest local reality shows, *The Real Housewives of Atlanta* and *Little Women of Atlanta*.

As James spoke on the phone he gave Kelly a couple eye rolls and hung up. "Jesse's free. He'll be at your home in a few hours. The auction doesn't start until nine." He checked his Breguet watch. It dripped in so many diamonds you could barely see the round dial. "I suggest you get home so you'll be ready."

She giggled, dashing out the room like a teenager going to her prom. She didn't want to go to an auction but if she had to, she'd be fine as hell doing it.

CHAPTER TWO

If people thought being styled by the best and having expensive clothes didn't make the person, they were a fool. After she'd dressed, Kelly stared in her bedroom mirror, not knowing who she was looking at. Oh, she could dress up with the best of them, but she'd never looked as stunning as she did tonight.

Blessed with a small waist, ample butt and womanalicious curves that went on for days and days, she filled out this garment with perfection.

The ladies at the boutique had done their thang and then some. They picked a cherry-red, spaghetti-strapped velvet dress. It was backless, with a sexy Crisscross tieback and a side slit that went so far up her thigh it should've been illegal.

Diamond chandelier earrings and clear, high-heeled sandals completed the look. No necklace, no bracelet. She understood why the women at the shop hadn't gone overboard with the accessories. In this dress, less was more.

Jesse had beat her hair like he was Mike Tyson. He'd put on all this mouse and gel and just slicked it straight back. She didn't know how he'd tamed all that weave, but her hair laid like a black river down her back. Once again, perfection. And just like the dress, Jesse went simple on her makeup to not take away from the rest of her look. He went light on the lipstick but added some fierce eyelashes because he said the focal point of a woman's face should always be her eyes, and since James thought her hazel eyes were so beautiful, she'd draw all the attention she could to them babies.

She looked so good she could murder a man with one glance, but she wasn't comfortable, that's for sure. The dress was hot as hell. Velvet in Atlanta in the middle of June? She'd be sweating more than Cecilia when the night was over with. The shoes could've been a size up because the straps pinched, but they'd remind her to walk more delicately. And her hair felt like it weighed a thousand pounds with all that gel, but she looked good.

She smiled in the mirror.

Damn good.

The auction was being held at the Art Museum and decorated to the hilt. Lights twinkled in the rafters and they had put aside an entire display hall with a massive stage at one end.

Kelly entered the room feeling like "Black Girl Magic" and everyone's gaze landed on *her*. She did a sexy twist as she moved and since the dress was constricting, she had no choice but to walk slow. Men gazed with desire in their eyes. Men who normally wouldn't even notice her in the room. But what Kelly loved was the women. Oh, she could see the envy rumbling through their veins.

Kelly sashayed past guests, patting her hair. She declined a glass of champagne by a passing male server in a silk vest and red bowtie, and scanned the place for James.

You couldn't miss him. He shined under the lights in a blue-black tux that hugged every muscle he had. His short blond locks laid plastered to his head with mousse as always. That man could be in a tornado and not one hair would be out of place. He must've used the same stuff Jesse had poured on her head. Shit her head was itching like a bitch, yet she couldn't pry her finger into it to scratch it.

Yep. Beauty definitely was pain.

No matter who was in the room, James stayed the center of attention and, as always, surrounded by a sea of desperate, fascinating women.

"Ah, Kelly." James rushed to her and did a double-take when he stopped. "Wow." His cheeks lost color as if he needed oxygen. "Man, you look amazing." He twirled her around and she felt his eyes on every inch of her. "Jesus. I don't think I've ever seen you so beautiful."

"Thanks." She gushed, getting the evil eye from the women he'd left across the room.

"I mean it. Your hair and that dress..." He swallowed. "Could make a man go crazy."

She grinned off the comment but hoped he wasn't just blowing smoke.

"You look fantastic too." She gestured to his glittery black bow tie. "Yet, you always do. You fit in anywhere."

"Man, you're beautiful." He kissed her cheek, breathing as if he were trying to inhale her. He held that kiss for what seemed like years, then finally let go.

"You smell good," she'd said it without realizing it. "Like the ocean."

"New cologne I'm trying out." His eyes slanted as he looked into hers. "Glad

it tempts you."
She half-chuckled, caught off-guard. "Did I say it did?"

"No." He parted his valentine lips that many women probably envied him for. "Your eyes did."

"My eyes, huh?" She looked away, the earrings brushing her neck. "Kind of inappropriate. Don't you think?"

He stared in a daze. "What?"

"How you're talking." She avoided eye contact. "I work for you, James. Remember?"

"Can I be honest when I say tonight, I don't care?"

She cleared her throat. "I think you should. Excuse me?" She gestured to a waitress with a tray of champagne. "I'll take one of these after all." She got a glass, and the server smiled as she left. "Suddenly my throat's dry."

James snickered. "I wonder why."

"Stop it," she whispered, licking the taste of the champagne from her lips. Oddly, it tasted like those sour apple gummy bears she loved. "How long you been here?"

"About an hour." He looked around. "I'm glad you rescued me. Damn." He tugged on his bow tie. "The women are relentless."

"Like you care."

"Hey, I know most men would dream to be me but you don't know what it's like having all these women chase you and they don't care about *me*." He straightened his jacket. "It's all about the money and status with them. I told you, I want a woman who doesn't care about that. Who sees more than a Fortune Five Hundred company and private jets when she looks at me."

"Am I supposed to feel sorry for you?"
He raised an eyebrow. "Come again?"

"James, you have everything anyone could want and you're complaining

because beautiful women want to be with you?"
"I don't like feeling like a piece of meat."
She laughed. "Then don't sign up for auctions."

He exhaled through his nostrils. "You know what I want, Kelly?" He rubbed up against her. "I want a woman I can talk to. Who I can relate to and who doesn't care about my money. Someone who really feels who I am and who cares about what I want. I want a woman who values love and not the shit I can buy her."

She gulped, the tight velvet trapping sweat.

"God." He gasped, gaze stroking her curves. "You look *so* good."

"This dress is not the most comfortable." She pulled at it, wiggling her hips.

"Maybe you should take it off."

She caught the sin in his eyes and he didn't even flinch. "James, stop. I mean it. We can't be talking like this."

"Why not?" he whispered, holding the curve of her back. "Something tells

me you like it."

She followed his gaze to her breasts and the imprint of her erect nipples shown through despite the lace bra.

"I'm right, huh?" He licked his lips. "Should've been talking like this a

long time ago."

"Are you drunk?"

"Maybe off of you."

"James." She huffed. "I can't bid on you if you're acting like this. Please,

you're making me uncomfortable. What's gotten into you?"

"Forget what's gotten into *me*." He caressed her ass. "Let's talk about what needs to get into *you*."

"James." She gently grabbed his hand and moved it. "Stop it."

"Are you uncomfortable because you want me to stop?" He dragged his fingertip over her cheek. "Or because you *don't*?"

Kelly stared at him, rescued by the boisterous voice that suddenly took over the room.

"James and Kelly!" Cecilia waddled through the doors in a botchy gold dress covered in sequins, her fat rolls screaming for mercy.

"Fuck." James rolled his eyes. "Shit. Just when I was hoping she wouldn't show up."

"Be nice." Kelly sipped from her glass.

Cecilia talked with some guests, laughing and sweating like she'd been hiking in the Amazon.

James scoffed. "I didn't know they made sequin dresses in eight X."

"Stop it, James." Kelly nudged him. "That's not nice. You're not supposed to talk about a woman's weight."

"Got nothing against big ladies, you know that." He squinted, ogling Cecilia. "There are plenty big girls I'd love to fuck, but Cecilia's just gross."

"Sh, she's coming over."

"Hello!" Cecilia spread out her flapping arms and grabbed Kelly into a soggy kiss. "Kelly, this dress. You look like the cover of *Vogue*."

"Thank you, Cecilia. You look great too."

"Ooh, thank, you girl." Cecilia did a turn. "James, what do you think?"

He gaped at the dress. "Uh—"

"He's at a loss for words, Cecilia. Meaning you look great."

"Oh, James is trying to play hard to get." Cecilia grinned, jabbing her finger into his stomach. "But, that's over tonight. I keep telling you we belong together and tonight you'll see it." She took a handkerchief from her sequin purse. "Woo, goodness. Is anyone else hot?" She dabbed her forehead. "I'm getting so many compliments on my dress tonight. I've lost a few pounds."

James nodded with a blank stare. "Is that so?"

"Yeah, in the stomach area."

James and Kelly exchanged glances.

"Been getting my steps in." Cecilia pinched James' cheek. "I will see you later, hot stuff." She pinched his butt.

He jumped. "Ow."

She winked at Kelly. "See you, Kelly."

"You too, Cecilia."

Cecilia waddled away.

"Steps my ass." James poked out his lips. "The only steps she takes are from the kitchen table to the refrigerator."

Kelly clenched her teeth. "*James*."

CHAPTER THREE

Many of the bachelors featured in the auction were business owners, but not nearly as successful or attractive as James. Several men raised a fair amount of money, and then finally it was time for James to take the stage.

A gaggle of women formed at the front of the crowd. Moments after the bidding started, Kelly could see that he was going to fetch the biggest amount by far. At least ten women, including Cecilia, were aggressively ramping up the dollar amounts.

Finally, all the women dropped out except the giddy Cecilia who acted like she had the game won.

Not so fast.

Kelly raised her paddle. "Six hundred thousand dollars."

"Six hundred thousand?" James wobbled, almost falling off the stage.

The auctioneer grabbed him. "Are you all right, Mr. Kris?"

James straightened his posture shooting daggers at Kelly.

She chuckled, mouthing, "You want me to win, don't you?"

But if they thought that stopped Cecilia, they were dead wrong. Her father might've just been the district attorney but her mother owned one of the most successful food chains in the nation, so Miss Cecilia had plenty of money to spare.

She raised her flabby arm. "Six hundred thousand and ten dollars!"

"Six hundred thousand and ten," the auctioneer announced. "Young lady, do you have another bid?"

Kelly looked around to see several people in the crowd turning to each other and whispering. James stood on stage sweating as if he were in front of a firing squad. She wasn't sure if it was because he wanted her to keep going or not.

Hell, he was a billionaire. He had the money.

"One million dollars!" Kelly raised her paddle.

James wobbled again, letting out a high-pitched screech that sounded like a woman giving birth.

"You heard her, folks," the auctioneer shouted. "A million dollars. Anyone want to top it?"

No one made a peep.

While shooting a look of murder at Kelly, Cecilia tossed her paddle to the marble floor, leapt out her chair and marched from the room.

"One million dollars for Mr. James Kris! Going once, going twice... sold!" The auctioneer banged his gavel. "At the highest bid of the night."

The crowd cheered and clapped and several women walked over to Kelly and hugged her. "Wow honey, you really want that date!"

They had no idea. Kelly was so high on adrenaline that she forgot she'd spent a ton of James' money.

Whoops.

He stepped off stage with his shoulders slumped and handsome face dragging on the floor.

"Don't say anything." Kelly lifted her hand before he whined. "You told me to spend whatever it took so you didn't have to go off with Miss Sweaty Pants."

"A million dollars?" He gasped.

"*Remember.*" Kelly sipped from her champagne glass. "It's for charity."

He straightened his posture, that confidence that made him so irresistible returning. "Did you see Cecilia's face?" He slapped his hands together, cackling. "If I were you, I'd hire me some security."

"I'm not worried about *her*. Maybe she'll finally get the hint that you're not interested."

He stood closer, pressing his chest muscles against her arm. "Thank you." He kissed her cheek again.

Kelly's knees knocked and her coochie turned a thousand flips. As she'd been bidding, focusing on claiming her man from all the other women, it was like a delicious sense of power. Something that she'd never known she could enjoy so much.

Now all she wanted was to make sure he followed through on the date. Getting to spend time with him outside of professional events was something she had always wanted.

"Well, you spent a good deal of money on me..." He rolled his eyes. "Or should I say, *I* spent the money."

She grinned.

"So where are we going to go on our date?" he asked.

"Oh, no. I saved you from Cecilia, so think of the date as thanking me. I'm expecting an incredible night out with an eligible bachelor, so you decide."

He scrutinized her dress again. Something about how he looked at her tonight just seemed different.

"Okay." He smiled. "Tomorrow night. I'll send my driver to pick you up and take you to my place. I promise I'll be worth the cost."

"One thing, though. No work talk," Kelly said. "Just two people getting together for a fun night. I don't want to feel like I'm out with my boss."

He winked. "Deal."

THE NEXT NIGHT, KELLY slipped on her burgundy cocktail dress that stopped a little below her knees. She had picked the white dress at first, but white seemed too innocent. The pink dress made her feel like a little girl going to her first recital, and the black dress was just way too suggestive for a first date with your boss.

The burgundy dress was perfect. It was flirty and chic. Not too long and not too short. Showed enough cleavage where it wasn't *too* revealing, but she didn't look like a nun either.

Boy did she want to wear that black dress, but with the way James was talking when he saw her in that red one last night, she doubted he could handle the black one.

She'd even struggled over what underwear to pick and settled on her black lace panties and matching bra. Definitely showed her slutty side, so what? He wasn't going to see it.

Right?

She enjoyed the ride to James' place in the back of the gigantic Lincoln. Course he'd sent the driver to her many times before, but not for a date. Usually it was to pick up his dry cleaning or gather documents for a meeting. Even the driver commented on how good she looked.

James opened the door dressed in indigo jeans and a tight crewneck, black T-shirt. "Wow, you look even more beautiful tonight."

"Yeah." She overlooked him and this wasn't what she expected. She thought she'd see the James she'd seen at the auction. A man in a suit and tie so polished he looked like he stepped off a movie screen.

Now, he still looked fantastic in casual clothes, but if she'd known he'd be in

jeans and a T-shirt she'd have thrown on a simple summer dress and called it a day.

"Are you all right?" he asked.

"I feel a bit overdressed."

"I'm sorry." He took her hand. "But I wanted to make you feel at home. I guess I should've said it was casual."

"No." She waved, trying to hide her disappointment. "I'm just glad to be here."

"Welcome." He showed her into the elegant, vintage foyer. "I'm just getting dinner ready. Hope you like risotto."

"I like anything that someone else cooks for me." Kelly laughed as she followed him through the long, oak hallways stacked with statues and paintings.

James turned toward her when he got to his rustic-style kitchen, the scent of onions and bouillon from the risotto making her even hungrier. "Well, I thought a fancy night out might be more to your liking, but I'd rather not be seen out on the town. If that's okay."

She understood, of course. If they were at a restaurant, the tabloids would take pictures, and then inevitably say something about him being out with one of his employees. This was more intimate anyway. Plus, she'd have him *all* to herself.

"Wine?" He got the bottle of Chateau Pauillac off the granite counter. "I had Gavino grab it from the wine cellar before he left."

"Ah." Kelly smelled the notes of black cherries and raspberries as he filled her glass. "Where is your faithful servant, anyway?"

"I gave him the night off." James walked to the island and handed her the glass. "I work Gavino like a dog and he never complains so he's well overdue for a break."

CHAPTER FOUR

"I always wondered why you have just one servant." She looked around at the exposed beams and stone walls. "With a house this big seems like you'd need a team."

"Gavino is all I want living here." He sipped his wine, batting his seductive lashes. "I hire out everyone else. You know me." He licked wine off his lips. "I like my privacy. You look incredible, Kelly."

The compliment shook her soul.

"I feel like I don't give you enough compliments, but I want you to know how much I appreciate you."

"James." She lowered her glass. "I'm just doing my job."

"No, you've gone above and beyond for me many times. And come on." He tilted his head, eyes narrowing. "You're not just an assistant, you're my friend. I've shared things with you I've never shared with anyone." He stood erect. "It's hard for me to trust people, so when I let someone into my circle, you best believe they're pretty special."

She smiled, cheeks tingling.

"You like the wine?"

"I love it."

He smirked. "Why are you smiling like that?"

"Having you serve me is something I can definitely get used to." She giggled.

"Milady." He bowed. "I aim to please."

They locked eyes, time standing still until she turned away. "So how's Davis?"

She almost choked on the wine. "Davis?"

"Yeah, your ex-boyfriend." He sat on the stool. "You remember him? The one who cheated on you and dumped you like an old tire."

"Oh, that Davis."

He squinted. "Yeah, that Davis."

"Always direct aren't you, James?"

"Well, I don't believe in bullshitting. You know that. What's going on with you two?"

"Who says anything is going on, and why are we suddenly talking about a man I haven't dated in two years?"

"Because he just came back into your life." He clasped his hands on the countertop. "Unless I'm wrong. I overheard you telling Claudia at the office that Davis called you and you met him for coffee." The veins in his cheeks pulsed. "Is that true?"

"James?" She held in a grin. "Are you jealous?"

"No, just wondering why you'd give a jerk like that the time of day."

"Look, he called me to check on me. He heard my mother got Covid and wanted to make sure she was all right."

"Why didn't he call *her* then?"

"I don't know, James, you'll have to ask him."

"But when you and Claudia were talking..." He closed his eyes. "You acted like you were open to seeing him again."

"Look, I know it's your company, but why don't you not eavesdrop on folks' conversations?" She huffed, turning away from him and leaning her back against the island. "Davis and I are over. Maybe a part of me considered giving him another chance, but then I remembered how much he hurt me."

"I remember too. I was the one who dried your tears, remember?"

She looked at him over her shoulder.

"The one who gave you time off because he hurt you so bad you couldn't think straight." He pressed his lips together. "You were going to leave Atlanta because you were so broken. I couldn't let you do that."

"I thought I had nothing here but Davis, and I was scared when it ended because I felt I always needed him."

"You're a beautiful, strong woman, Kelly. You don't need any man."

She smiled.

"But I am your friend and Davis doesn't deserve you."

"It's done with Davis, okay?" She swung back around and set her glass on the counter. "I told him not to call me again."

His face blushed with bliss. "Really?"

"Yes. You're right. I deserve better and I told him that."

"Well." He patted the counter. "I'm glad."

"Yeah, but I don't understand why, James. Why do you care?"

He smirked as he finished his wine. "Do you want another glass?"

She smiled. "Sure."

KELLY DIDN'T HAVE TO lift a finger all evening. James treated her like royalty throughout dinner, and he had some skills with making risotto. He was completely different compared to how he was at the office, and it was really nice to see this side of him.

All night they shot the breeze, talking about stuff you'd discuss with an old friend you knew for decades. He shared more about his family. She'd never asked about them much, figuring it wasn't her business. It warmed her how easily he opened up. In return, she shared her professional ambitions and where she hoped to be in ten years.

By the time dessert was on the table, a delectable chocolate lava cake, Kelly's head was swimming being so close to him.

"You know, I didn't expect you to be such a skilled cook," she said.

"I gotta confess. I didn't make this cake."

"Either way, I'm enjoying myself very much."

He slipped cake onto his fork and held it to her mouth.

She grinned. "Ooh yes, feed me." She parted her mouth, and James slipped the fork into it.

Kelly glided her lips across the utensil, cleaning every crumb as she did.

James gaped, his hand stuck in midair.

Kelly froze, overtaken by a sexual desire so strong it would've knocked her off her feet had she been standing.

He scooped more cake onto the fork and put it between her lips.

As she licked off the tines, she saw his eyes eagerly watching her. It was unexpected, but intensely erotic. "More," she demanded.

He smiled, caving to her demand.

"I like this." She licked the salty frosting from her mouth. "Telling you what to do. Controlling you."

There was a warm flush through her body that had nothing to do with the wine. And tension was slowly building between them. Now all she had to do was figure out how to make him see her as more than just an employee. All of her thoughts slid towards seducing him somehow, and the reaction to him feeding her gave her an idea.

She needed to take control. Maybe that was exactly what he was craving. And she could definitely handle it.

"Let's sit in the living room." She handed him her wine glass.

Obediently, he led her towards the massive, wooded living room that resembled the interior of a lavish cabin.

The room was warm and as they sat down close to each other she could see that he was expectant about what she might say next. It was easy to decide what to tell him to do.

Now was the *real* test.

Would he happily obey her commands, or would he resist?

"I loved dinner." She propped her elbow on the back of the fluffy white couch. "But for the money I spent, you could take it up a couple of notches."

"You mean the money *I* spent." He laughed. "But what did you have in mind?"

He had always been a total alpha male in the boardroom. So she wondered if she could actually tame the beast. After all, he seemed to enjoy being submissive right now.

"I think a foot massage would be nice." She wiggled her toes in her high-heeled sandals. "Take off my shoes."

With a poker face that gave nothing away, James moved onto the floor in front of her.

She couldn't believe her boss, the man she would marry in a hot minute if he looked at her long enough, kneeled in front of her, ready to massage her feet. But there he was, eager to follow her commands.

His massage skills were remarkable. Every time he touched her toes, it sent an electric jolt through her entire body. "That's really nice." She closed her eyes as she moaned.

"You got pretty toes, Kelly."

She opened her eyes, panties soaked already.

"Pretty enough to suck." He slipped his fingertips between her toes, the motion reminding her of being fingered.

He smiled, his hands making her shiver. And his attitude was that of total submission, like he was enjoying being told what to do.

How ironic. He spent his entire life telling others what to do, and within moments she molded him into her slave. She'd heard that guys who were dominant in everyday life sometimes were submissive in the bedroom.

She couldn't wait to test that theory.

CHAPTER FIVE

"**K**iss my toes. Worship them." She loved it when guys paid attention to her feet and with his skillful hands, Kelly hoped his mouth was just as good.

He nibbled on them at first, then took them deep into his hot, wet mouth, gliding his fat tongue on the ball of her foot.

"Oh." Her nipples hardened. "That feels so good."

She loved getting her toes sucked. The spit in between the creases, the way a man's tongue tickled the nerves at the bottom of her foot. Women who didn't get foot loving didn't know what they were missing. It always got Kelly hotter than anything else.

G-spot times one thousand.

Seeing his pink tongue between her brown toes drove her crazy.

"James?"

"Hmm." He sucked her big toe like a baby with a bottle.

"Have you ever been with a black chick before?"

He opened his eyes with her toe resting on his bottom lip. "What?"

She wiggled her toes against his mouth. "Have you ever been with a black woman before?"

"Yeah." He scoffed and went back to sucking.

"Who?"

"What difference does it make? I've been with a lot of black women."

She smirked. "How many?"

"I don't know. I've dated many women, Kelly. Women from all over the world and all walks of life."

"What black chicks?"

He groaned, still giving her foot tongue action.

"Who?"

"Plenty," he mumbled with her middle toes in his mouth.

She tapped her foot on his nose. "*Who?*"

"Mercy."

"Wait, Mercy *Stevens?*" She sat up. "*The* Mercy Stevens? The so-called love of your life?"

"No, I *thought* she was the love of my life."

"The woman you talk about constantly because she broke your heart? The one you dated for almost five years? The only woman on this earth you *ever* proposed to? That Mercy Stevens?"

He licked drool from between her toes. "That would be her."

"For real? You never said Mercy was black."

"I didn't think I had to."

"You didn't have to but I'm black and she's black and when you said all this other shit about her it didn't cross your mind to mention it?"

"Guess I didn't think it was important. Did I pass your litmus test, or I gotta write names of every black woman I've fucked?"

She held in a grin, feeling silly. "Sorry. But I wanted to know."

"Have you ever been with a white guy?"

She shook her head and a sly smile covered his lips.

"I take it you enjoy hearing that," she said.

"What man doesn't want to be the first? Now can we get on with this or are there anymore awkward questions you want to ask?"

She stuck out her chin. "Proceed, *slave*."

"Slave, huh? I got your slave." He kissed her feet, sending another wave of electricity through her pussy.

"Mm." Kelly rocked, fighting her moans as James went to town on that big toe.

When he finished with one foot, he swapped to the next, giving it the same wonderful attention with his lips and tongue.

"Damn..." Kelly sighed. "I had no idea you enjoyed this."

"Neither did I." He laughed.

"I didn't say you could talk." She snapped, and he quickly bowed his head and kissed her foot again. "Let's see how that mouth does somewhere else."

For once, she wasn't holding back how much she wanted him. After all, this might be her only chance.

It was time to push the limits.

Kelly had always had a fantasy of her powerful boss between her legs, servicing her. She spread her legs and quickly pulled her panties aside, exposing her dripping slit. "Lick me. *Slowly*."

James nodded and moved up her body, kissing her thighs. When his lips

touched her pussy, she gasped from the sensation. He eagerly slid his wet tongue down and then slowly back up, nibbling at her pussy lips.

And he was marvelous at it, taking her cues without hesitation.

Finally, he looked up and grabbed her panties. "May I?"

Kelly nodded and let him slip them down her legs. He dove back in and continued his oral work. Her clit twitching with every swipe of his talented tongue.

"Oh my God. James..."

Yes, yes, after all these years of dreaming and praying. Her boss, James Kris himself, licked her pussy better than any man ever had. She was desperate for more and ached to see him naked.

Closing her legs and pushing his head away, she commanded him to stand up. "Take off your shirt. Slowly."

He raised his shirt, exposing his rippling abs. Most men would've died to have James' Adonis physique.

"Now your pants."

He nodded, each command met with gleeful obedience. It was like having a wonderful new toy that had an incredible body, and when he slid his shorts down, his delicious cock emerged.

She couldn't wait to use it for her pleasure.

"Take my dress off." Kelly turned and James unzipped her, slowly brushing away the straps of her dress until it laid on the floor. "Fold it up and put it over there."

"Yes, Ma'am." He followed the command and returned.

"Unhook my bra and set it and my panties with my dress."

James just stood there, his eyes wide as soccer balls.

In the heat of the moment she had forgotten she was actually standing in front of him buck naked.

"Jesus." He sucked his bottom lip. "You're so damn hot, Kelly. I knew you had a great body, but it's out of this world."

She beamed, gripping her waist. "I work out sixteen hours a week. Low carbs, low sugar and as much protein as my body will take."

He blushed. "It's definitely paying off."

"Now shut up." She snapped her fingers. "Get on your knees again and kiss my feet, slave."

James dropped and kissed both feet obediently. He knelt there in front of her, obviously waiting for another command. The power was a massive aphrodisiac.

"What now, Mistress?"

"Your bedroom. Show me."

Kelly got the condoms from her purse and followed him with a smirk.

CHAPTER SIX

James led Kelly to his bedroom and the minute she stepped in it felt like entering another dimension. Just like the rest of his home, it was contemporary chic with rustic charm. Despite all the money he had, he hadn't drenched the rooms in obnoxious luxury, but he kept things simple and had what he needed and not much else. That's what she liked about James. He might've had all the money in the world, but he didn't throw it away.

He batted his eyes like a little boy begging his mom for a piece of candy. "Do you like it, Mistress?"

Kelly stuck her nose in the air. "It'll do."

He smiled.

She didn't care if his bedroom was in a swamp. She only wanted one thing.

To enjoy him like she'd always fantasized about. "Okay, lie down on the bed."

He stretched over the king-sized mattress with the lavender linen sheets. The sight of him submissively lying there, ready for her to enjoy, was simply too much.

She looked down at him. "If you're not a good boy, then this is what you're going to get."

She climbed on the bed and pushed her foot against his cock and balls with just enough force to make him whimper.

He grimaced. "What was that for?"

"I want to make sure you know who's in charge."

"Trust me, I do."

She grinned but didn't want to torture him *too* much. James had proven he was her submissive already. Now it was time to enjoy him.

She got the condom and maneuvered it over his shaft.

"Mm." He closed his eyes, laying with his arms folded behind his head. "Even that feels good."

"Does it?"

"Yeah, your fingers are like magic."

"The pussy's even better." Crouching down she quickly slid his thick,

pulsating dick up her dripping cunt, the rubber causing a little friction as she eased him inside her. When he tried to touch her, she batted his hands away. "No touching. This is all for me. You're going to be my fuck toy."

A relaxing smile came over James' face as Kelly moved slowly, feeling his cock enter her fully and massage her most sensitive spots.

She moaned, his enormous shaft stretching her pussy. "God, you feel good." The fact she was on top of him, riding the man she'd wanted for so long was beyond anything she'd imagined when she bid on him at the auction.

"You feel amazing." James roughly squeezed her breasts as she arched her back to push them further into his hands.

"Pinch my nipples."

He obeyed, taking the brown nubs in his fingertips and squeezing them hard enough to make her wince with pain. Just one touch was enough to send a massive surge of erotic need through her pussy and she contracted hard, pushing herself down onto him as a delicious shiver of ecstasy crippled her body.

"Fuck me harder." She rode his cock, which was now drenched in her pussy juice. "Pound me!" She rocked, tits bouncing so hard they made a slapping noise. "I want you from behind. Make me come over and over."

Kelly slid off him and got onto all fours. James seized her hips, thrusting back into her. His member making her pussy stretch more, this time with the depth of his strokes.

The control he had was incredible, and she could tell he was trying hard to please her with no thought of himself.

Her body shivered through another orgasm, and she lost count of how many times his talented body made her explode. Whenever he seemed to come close to an orgasm, he would slow down, cruelly teasing her.

"More." She bounced back on his dick. "Harder, James!"

He pulled out of her with a gasp. "Kelly... you're driving me crazy. I'm so close."

She had an idea. A way to pay him back for fucking her so well. And also a way to establish that she was firmly in charge of his sexual pleasure. Shoving him down to the bed, his rigid cock stood straight up, slick with her juices all over it. Taking him in her hand, she stroked him.

Within moments his back arched, and he gasped loudly. "Oh, God! Yes! Please, make me come, Kelly!"

"No." She stopped. "You're not allowed to come, dirty boy."

James grimaced, wrinkles filling his forehead.

"I can feel you." She squeezed his throbbing dick. "You're right on the edge, aren't you? But I have control."

He twisted his red face, looking like he would have a heart attack.

"Having this power over your body is exciting me just as much as having you inside."

"Oh fuck, please, Kelly. This is torture. Come on."

"Shut up." She stroked him more.

He rolled his body with her rhythm, abs heaving and his breath in desperate pants. Feeling his body tighten up, she stopped again.

A small bead of cum appeared inside the condom, and then more dribbled out. "Uh-oh. Bad boy. We need a new rubber."

"No, please. I want to feel you, skin-to-skin. I'm safe, Kelly. You can trust me."

Of course she trusted James or she wouldn't have been at his place. Actually, she hated using condoms but safety always came first.

"I thought you wanted to use one to be sure—"

"Sure of what?" He touched her hand. "I know the type of woman you are, and you don't sleep around."

She smiled, removed the soaked condom, and squeezed his balls while blowing lightly on his shaft.

He moaned from the base of his throat. "Please, don't stop."

Just as he would relax a bit, she'd stroke him again.

He groaned, clenching the sheet, his muscles flexing from reaction.

"Ah." He erupted like a fountain, spurting straight up in a thick stream and splattering onto his stomach, hips and her hand. He let out a masculine, primal scream with every ejaculation, and there were *several* that followed.

Kelly stroked him to completion. She knew his cock was probably insanely sensitive. Still, the control was absolute, and he obeyed her commands not to touch her, even though she could tell he was very uncomfortable not being able to.

She released him and he shuddered, gasping with relief.

James went onto his knees and kissed her naked thighs. "That was incredible."

Stroking his hair, Kelly knew that their relationship had changed. Now that she'd seen his submissive side, things were going to be very different. Especially around the office.

The best part of the evening was how he took her into his arms and held her. They spent the night talking and sharing more than they ever had before. She wanted to ask James just how he felt about her, but when he kissed her, interrupting her doubtful thoughts, she knew she didn't have to. He cared for her deeply. Every touch, every way he looked at her told her everything she needed to know.

KELLY WALKED INTO THE office Monday morning feeling like she owned the world. She exchanged some light conversation with Claudia, wondering if she could tell Kelly and James had fucked each other's brains out, then Kelly slipped into his office and closed the door.

James just sat behind his desk with that sly grin and once again, he didn't have to say anything for her to know how he felt.

"I got you something." She placed the little package on his desk. "Ready for Round Two?"

"Two?" He gaped. "How about Round One Hundred? I think I had sex more times the other night with you than I've had in a month."

She laughed as she slid upon his desk and crossed her legs so he could see up her skirt. "I'm not wearing any panties."

"Now, Miss Banks." He wagged his finger at her. "This isn't appropriate."

"If you think *that's* not appropriate, wait and see what I'm about to do to you right here in the office."

Grinning, James opened the box. "What the hell is this?" He pulled out the metal, penis-shaped contraption.

"Really?" Kelly giggled. "You don't know? You're greener than I thought."

"Seriously, what is this?" He held it up, examining it like it was an alien being.

Kelly leaned over the desk, her boobs hanging from her blouse. "It's a cock cage. I put it on you, lock it, and I keep the key." She leaned back up, shaking her foot. "And I can do anything I *want*."

"Damn, girl. I didn't know you were into this kind of stuff."

"Guess it's a good thing I bought you at the auction or you'd never know."

He blushed.

"You are all right with this, aren't you?"

"Oh, yes, Mistress. I just wish I'd known about this side of you sooner."

She sashayed around his desk, stopping in front of him. "If you liked the other night, you ain't seen nothing yet." She yanked his chair, turned it toward her and snatched the cock cage from his hand.

"Wait." He chuckled as she undid his pants. "Kelly, what are you doing?"

"It's 'Mistress' to you, slave. Now be a good boy and wear this for me."

"Kelly, we can't." He grabbed her hands, laughing nervously. "Kelly, come on now. Come on."

"Shut up." She yanked down his zipper and knelt in front of him.

"I don't believe this." He laughed. "You're something else."

Kelly wiggled her eyebrows. "Be a good boy for mama."

"Okay, but just tell me... is this thing gonna hurt?"

"Yes." She pulled his pants down. "And you're gonna love it."

THE END

To receive book announcements subscribe to Stacy's mailing list: Mailing List[1]

SAMPLE OF BILLIONAIRE IN THE CARIBBEAN BELOW

CHAPTER ONE

Los Angeles, California

L "Are you fucking kidding me?" Twenty-nine-year-old Samantha Vanguard snatched her nightgown from the dresser drawer. "You can't pull this shit on me, Kendrick, not again. You said you were coming to Barbados with me and Kay. We were gonna make a vacation out of it."

"I'm sorry but I couldn't get the time off," said the sexy yellow bone with freckles painting his face. You could tell everything Kendrick was thinking just by the lines in his forehead and judging by what Sam saw in his face this morning, he was once again full of shit. "Besides, this is a business trip for you guys. What would it look like for me to tag along?"

"This is bullshit." She threw her nightgown on top of the other clothes in her suitcase. "You must've known before now that you wouldn't be able to go yet you just tell me right before we gotta get on the plane? All you think about is J&M."

"I'm a supervisor at J&M, remember? I can't just leave town when they need me."

"You work for a damn warehouse where they ship out pies all day. It's not like someone would've died if you weren't around for five days." She got powder and deodorant from the adjacent bathroom and walked back into the bedroom. "You're just doing this to kiss up to Mr. Sinclair."

"Call it what you want, but bending over backwards when my boss needs me to is how I got my position. I'm not apologizing for that. Wow." He crossed his toned arms. "I'm thirty, Sam. The youngest supervisor J&M has ever had. You think that would've happened if I hadn't 'kissed up' as you say?"

"I'm proud of you but I'm tired of your job interfering with everything we want to do in our personal lives."

"What about *your* job?" He laughed. "Miss Big Time Agent from TriSun Advertising? Your schedule is pretty grueling too."

"But I still make time for us."

"Sam." He moved in behind her, gripping her shoulders with those pale hands. "I love you, honey."

She groaned, tired of hearing the words but seeing no action that met it

lately.

"Look." He turned her around and took her hands. "I promise we'll go on our own trip, but again, you and Kay got business to take care of. I don't want to be a distraction."

"I just feel like we're drifting farther apart every day."

"We've had a hectic three years. It can take a toll on a relationship." He pulled her thin body to him, his embracing swallowing her. "You moved in with me, you became the head sales agent at TriSun last year, and I moved up at J&M. It's been a lot of changes, babe." He stroked the large, luxurious waves of her golden-brown Brazilian extensions. "But, like I keep saying, we'll look back on these sacrifices and be glad we made them." Kendrick put on that snake oil salesman smile and pushed his nose to hers. "Think about when we get married and have kids. We'll be set, Sam. Won't have to struggle for nothing. Isn't that what we want for our children? To not have to grow up like we did?"

She dropped her head. "Yeah, but—"

He lifted her chin. "Anyway, all on your mind should be this big client you're trying to snag."

"Ain't that the truth?" She folded clothes to fit them into the suitcase. "Kay and I *have* to nail this dude if we ever want to move up at TriSun. I don't want to be a sales agent my entire career, going out and chasing the clients, so the higher-ups at the company reap all the benefits. I want to sit in the big chair one day, running that company and making the final decisions."

"Stop worrying. If anyone can get this big client, you can." He smiled through his slender cheeks. "After all, would Mr. Huffman be sending you to the Caribbean if he didn't think you could complete the deal?

This client must be big shit to demand you guys meet him in another country."

"He lives in New York but he's vacationing in Barbados and he made it more than

clear if we wanted to meet him, we needed to go where he's at. Huffman's so desperate for this deal, he'd have sent us anywhere."

Kendrick smirked. "At least you get a free trip out of it."

"Seriously, babe. We're the only black women at the agency, and we don't

wanna fuck up the biggest assignment we've gotten. We don't want them to have any reason to doubt us. You know how it is."

"Oh, I *do*." He chuckled. "You're talking to the only black guy at J&M besides the janitor for the last ten years. Not a lot of us at the top of these companies so we gotta work our asses off to stay around." He strolled to the other side of the bed and sat. "That's why you should understand why I can't just drop things and go to Barbados right now. But, I promise we'll go on a trip soon, sweetie. Just chill and rock with me, okay? It'll be worth it."

THE SECOND SAM AND Kay stepped off the plane in Bridgetown, Barbados, Sam felt guilty. Why? Because no way in the world should she be so gloomy when she was actually on the trip of a lifetime. Most people would kill to be sent to the Caribbean for free to stay in a gorgeous, beachside resort hotel.

Speaking of the hotel, it was all that and then some. One thing about TriSun is they knew how to treat their employees. They didn't stash them away in some raggedy hotel in the ghetto. No. They were right in the upper crust of Bridgetown in a multi-floor hotel surrounded by a stunning beach that stretched for miles and sat right in the middle of the best shopping malls and restaurants.

In the prime spot for tourists, the location guarded you from the less desirable elements of the city.

Sam had heard horror stories about how local criminals and scammers made tourists' lives a nightmare. She had read up on what places to go to and those to avoid. Still, no amount of preparation pushed away that tiny smidge of fear that something bad could happen.

Here she and Kay were, two attractive American women traveling on their own. Sam would do her best for them not to end up on a milk carton somewhere.

"I don't care what you say..." Kay told Sam as the women followed the black baggage porter into the roomy, pristine elevator. "I'm getting some dick tonight."

"Girl." Sam nudged her, avoiding the awkward stare from the porter as they got into the elevator. "Be quiet," she whispered.

"Girl, I don't care about this fool." Kay took out her mirror and examined her face.

"I need some dick. I haven't been fucked in a month." She turned to the porter, who kept his eyes straight, clearing his throat. "A damn month. I'm not used to that like you, Sam."

"Excuse me?"

"Please." Kay stuffed her mirror in her purse. "The only thing that's been hitting your pussy lately is the water when you get in the shower." She laughed. "We know damn well Kendrick's workaholic ass ain't been down there lately."

"Would you shut up?" Sam faked a smile at the porter. "I apologize."

"It's fine, Miss." He kept his lanky body erect, African features blushing from awkwardness. "Where are you ladies from?"

"Los Angeles," Kay said all loud, smacking gum. "Say, you're pretty cute. I love me a tall chocolate man."

Sam dropped her head. "Oh, God."

"Uh, thank you." The porter plastered on a smile, shifting his eyes left and right. "But I'm married."

Kay looked him over. "I don't see a ring."

"Kay." Sam pulled her away from the poor man as the elevator stopped. "He's trying to let your ass down easy."

The porter snickered as he pushed the luggage cart into the hall.

"Keep your mind off getting booty and on business," Sam told Kay as they walked through the sparkling white hallway and floor of octagon tiles. "We gotta do all we can to get the Hart Baldwin account."

"Hart Baldwin this, Hart Baldwin that." Kay rolled her eyes. "Girl, this is Barbados. How many times you think we'll get to come here and with everything paid for us?" She winked at a guy when they passed. "We'll get the account."

"No joke. Hart is the biggest fish you and I could land. Don't forget we're being held to a higher standard than those white folks we work with." Sam huffed as they got to room 309. "They're just waiting for us to blow this."

"Mr. Huffman isn't like that." Kay spit her gum into the wastebasket and the porter grimaced as he opened the door. "He values us. If he hadn't, he wouldn't have hired us."

"You mean if TriSun hadn't gotten such heat for years for not having any
minorities there, he wouldn't have hired us."

"Ewe." Kay frowned. "You're always so negative. If we weren't good workers would we have been there for five years?"

"I know we're damn good workers but don't fool yourself that they think of us like they do the other employees."

"Okay, ladies." The porter placed their luggage into the room and came out, rubbing his hands. "I hope you enjoy your stay and let us know if you need anything else."

"Oh, we *will*." Kay squinted to read his name badge. "Nice to meet you, Marcus. I'm Kay." She flapped her hand out at him.

"Nice to meet you." He barely touched her hand as if he thought she had a disease. "I hope you enjoy your stay." He looked back and forth between them, smiling. "Yes, yes." He bounced on his heels.

"Oh." Sam laughed. "Sorry." She took a ten out of her purse. "Here you go. Thanks."

He smiled, folding the bill. "I'll see you."

"Definitely come back and see me, baby!" Kay waved at him.

Marcus grimaced at her over his shoulder and continued walking.

CHAPTER TWO

"You scared that man to death." Sam chuckled, closing her purse.

"You gave him a ten? All he did was bring the bags up, which is his job."

"Ah, how soon we forget life outside of corporate America. I remember not too long ago *we* were living off tips." Sam carried her suitcase to the second bed by the window, overlooking the tourists in the pool area. "I'm so tired I don't even feel like unpacking."

"Stop acting like an old lady. " Kay took out a container of Africa's Best Hair Conditioner. "Girl, this humidity is killing my hair." She rubbed conditioner in her palms and spread it on her natural, shoulder-length hair before tying it into a slick ponytail. "How are things with you and Kendrick? He still hasn't put a ring on it?"

"No." Sam sat on the bed and kicked off her flip-flops. "And I'm wondering if I want him to."

Kay's eyes went wide as she looked back at Sam through the mirror. "For real?"

"I love him, but I'm sick of being the only one fighting for this relationship. All he cares about is his career, but makes me feel guilty about mine. He actually seemed happy I didn't get the manager position at Ace Advertising."

"Don't say that. I'm sure he was as crushed as you were. I'm sorry you didn't get it. Man." Kay shook her head. "I thought you had it in the bag. They loved you in the interviews."

"I just don't understand it. One minute I had them eating out of my hand and they couldn't wait to bring me on and the next minute I'm not right for the company?" She stroked the multicolor bedspread. "Never made sense."

"Well, what did Kendrick say they said exactly when he took the call?"

"That I wasn't right for the job after all but didn't go into any details. How could I be right one minute and not the next? You don't think someone from TriSun found out I was talking to Ace and did something?"

"Girl, no telling." Kay turned from the mirror and leaned back on the dresser. "Ace is TriSun's biggest competitor after all, so I'm sure they wouldn't have been too keen on you leaving to go there. But I highly doubt Ace would've listened to anyone at TriSun."

"If only I hadn't been in the shower and missed the call." Sam dropped her shoulders. "Just those few minutes changed everything. I wanted to call them back and convince them to give me another shot but it didn't feel right."

"Fuck 'em." Kay got lotion from her bag and sat on the other bed. "You don't need to beg anyone for a job. Besides, once we get the Hart Baldwin account, we'll probably get promotions. Are you nervous?"

"About meeting Hart? No." Sam scoffed, lying through her teeth. "He's just a potential client like the others we've dealt with."

"Yeah, but this is Hart Baldwin." Kay lotioned her legs. "He's not just anyone he owns Baldwin Industries, and last time I checked that was the biggest food distributor in the world." She whistled. "And he's only thirty-five and a very *handsome* thirty-five I might add."

"It's easy to own a company when your daddy handed it down to you. Trust me, I'm not intimidated by Hart Baldwin or his money. To me he's just another rich brat who gets everything he's always wanted."

"Yeah but that rich brat is the biggest fish TriSun has ever chased." Kay spread lotion on her other leg. "Don't forget he's worked with some of the best ad companies in the world, so it's a big fuckin' deal if he chooses us. He alone could change both our careers, Sam. Besides, he isn't bad to look at."

Sam rolled her eyes as she stood. "Is sex always on your mind?"

"Stop fronting." Kay snickered. "You were drooling over him when he appeared in that *Forbes* article the same way I was. Oh, he is *so* hot." She shuddered. "Those gorgeous, hazel eyes and that accent. Ooh, girl. I love me a British accent."

"Please be professional when we meet with him tomorrow." Sam got her nightgown and some panties out of her suitcase. "We can't let anything spoil this, Kay."

She rolled her eyes. "For women to make waves in this business, you gotta flirt a bit."

"Well, not me." Sam headed to the bathroom. "I'm taking a shower."

"Cool. I'll get in after you." Kay jumped up, swerving her shapely hips. "And then we can get on to the clubs."

"Uh-uh. No. I'm not going anywhere but to this bed. I'm so tired I don't even wanna eat."

"But it's only five-thirty. You can't go to bed this early."

Sam went into the bathroom. "Watch me." She set her stuff on the sink as Kay walked in.

"We're in the freaking Caribbean, Sam. Did you see all those hot men we passed in the lounge? Honey, this is the islands! We gotta have some fun."

"Having strange men sneak roofies in my drink the minute my back is turned is *not* fun." Sam turned on the shower. "You can go out, but please don't act crazy and make sure you get some rest. Can't have you looking a hot mess in front of Baldwin tomorrow." Sam prodded Kay out of the bathroom and finished undressing. "You hear me, Kay?"

"Yes, I hear you," she snapped back. "Someone needs to remind you, you're not dead yet, Sam. So stop acting like it."

Sam snickered as she stepped into the shower.

CHAPTER THREE

Sam pulled at her Vera Wang blazer as she and Kay entered the hotel lounge the next morning to meet with Hart Baldwin. "I don't see him yet."

"I told him to meet for breakfast at nine." Kay walked beside Sam, swinging her Gucci purse. "He's probably late on purpose so he can make an entrance."

"Entrance my ass. No one has time to be waiting all day."

"This is Hart Baldwin we're talking about." Kay wiggled her eyebrows. "We'll wait until Christmas if we have to."

They sat in the spacious booth right beside the window, where Sam could see the entire pool area.

A muscular, deep-chocolate server with pearly-white teeth asked to take their orders. They declined telling him to come back later. He flirted with a smile and left.

"Damn, he's fine." Kay licked her lips. "I don't know how I'm gonna keep my mind out the gutter with all this sexy ass chocolate around."

"Stop," Sam muttered.

"He was flirting too." Kay's eyes lit up. "Did you see him? I think he likes me."

"These hotels tell these workers to flirt with tourists so they can distract you from how overpriced the food is."

"You look amazing," Kay said. "That suit is fire."

Sam looked down at her beige pantsuit and blazer. "It's new." She fixed the top as best she could to cover her cleavage. "It's a little low-cut but not too much, is it?"

Kay smirked. "Depends on who you ask."

Sam loved pantsuits because they represented power and femininity. While some women in the corporate world felt being feminine was a hindrance instead of an attribute, Sam reveled in being a woman and felt it gave her an edge with male clients.

Back in the day, nothing she wore made her feel good about herself. She'd always been self-conscious because she didn't have the massive curves the other women in her family did.

You could park a car on her mother's ass.

Sam had always been tall and slender with little titties and barely a bump for an ass

and her mother teased her for her lack of curves more than anyone. She always joked that Sam looked like a wannabe WNBA player.

But fast forward past those awkward teen years, and Sam loved her body now. After all, that "boyish figure" didn't seem so bad when she looked amazing in a string bikini.

"Cross your fingers Hart likes us." Kay snatched Sam's hand. "But I got confidence in you. If you can't get Hart to sign on with us, no one can."

"Hey, I'm not doing this by myself." Sam smiled. "We're in this together and we'll get this deal. No matter what it takes."

But Hart wasn't easy to please. He was a shark, which is how he got to be so successful. Sure, Hart's daddy had handed him Baldwin Industries, but since his father passed, Hart had become a business tyrant, buying up food companies left and right.

He was the worst type of client; savvy with a manipulative streak. Even Mr. Huffman warned Sam to watch out for Hart's tricks because he would do anything to lowball you on a deal.

"Ooh, shit." Kay jumped at attention. "There he is. Man, he's so fine."

Sam looked up, meeting Hart's unapologetic gaze. His hazel eyes shined brighter as he stared upon Sam as if he'd been on fire and she was a hose full of water.

Glowing in elegance, he looked just like he did in the magazines. Flawless vanilla skin, as if he used every skin product on the market to get it looking that good. Luscious, pouty lips and boy could the man dress.

Hart wasn't a "he-man" with meaty biceps and six-pack abs but he had the right amount of muscles and was more toned than any athlete. He could make a paper bag look sexy.

Wearing a crisp, white dress shirt and black slacks, he glided toward the table, not even acknowledging Kay.

Hell, Sam had forgotten about her, too.

Hart's brown eyebrows lowered over his eyes, suggesting seeing Sam overwhelmed him. "*Hello.*" His sexy Cockney accent forced its way through his raspy voice. "I'm Hart Baldwin and you are?" He extended his hand across the table to Sam when Kay jumped out the booth.

"Mr. Baldwin!" She snatched his hand, almost pulling the man over.

"God," Sam muttered, dropping her head.

"It's wonderful to meet you, sir. I'm Kay Hinsley from TriSun. I'm the one you spoke to on the phone."

Hart looked back and forth at Sam while shaking Kay's hand. "It's uh, nice to meet you, but I thought I was meeting Sam too. Where is he?"

"He?" Sam grimaced.

"Hello." Hart passed Kay and grabbed Sam's hand. "Well, you're a lush, aye?"

Sam grimaced. "Excuse me?"

He grinned. "In Britain, it means you're beautiful."

"Well in America it means you're a drunk."

"I'm Hart Baldwin and if you don't know who I am, trust me, you'll want to." He kissed her hand, causing Sam's pussy to twitch.

Kay gaped.

"Mm. You smell remarkable." Hart gripped Sam's hand tighter. "I didn't catch your name."

"Uh," Kay said. "Mr. Baldwin, Sam—"

"Where *is* Sam?" He stood erect. "You said he'd be here at nine. It's very unprofessional for him to keep me waiting. You think I have nothing better to do? Get the bloke on the phone, aye? I'd love to make a deal with TriSun but right now I'm not impressed by him at all." Hart slid into the booth next to Sam and she gaped at Kay, who shrugged.

"*Now*..." Hart put his arm on the back of the booth behind Sam. "While I wait for someone who obviously has better things to do than talk business with me, I can get to know *you* better. What is your name?"

Sam swallowed. "I'm Sam."

He gaped with his mouth wide open. "Uh... come again?"

"*I'm* Sam Vanguard." She smiled. "Samantha. Glad you're ready to talk business because I sure am."

"Um." He glanced at Kay and back at Sam. "You're not at all what I expected." He

gave her the once-over. "Sam Vanguard. Your name sounds like an old man."

She chuckled. "Well, I'm definitely not one."

"No." He swallowed, his gaze dropping to her cleavage. "Forgive me. I have to get over the fact that you're not a bloke."

"I hope it's not a problem because TriSun is very interested in your business and we think we can further expand your visibility. We offer several packages as my boss Mr. Huffman has already explained to you. I'm prepared to explain everything but I'm determined not to leave Barbados until you're a part of the TriSun family." She sat back, smiling. "How does that sound?"

Hart propped his elbow on the table, rubbing his smooth, angular face. "Wow. I just... you're not what I expected."

Kay rolled her eyes and finally sat down.

"You're so young." Hart moaned, biting his lip. "So attractive."

Sam blinked, and she suddenly felt feverish, as if her blood pressure was rising. One of her rules was to never get involved with a client. Of course, she had a boyfriend, but even without one it just wasn't right. She wanted to rise in the ranks as much as anyone, but not if it meant being on her back.

She wiggled in the seat, nipples throbbing. It had been easier to say that before, but she'd never met a man like Hart Baldwin. And Kay was right. The man was *fine*.

"What do you say?" Sam clasped her hands. "Do you know what you want already? I'll be glad to go into more detail."

"Oh I definitely know what I want." He narrowed his eyes, chuckling.

"We also have some presentations we've prepared," Kay said. "We'd love to show them to you. Remember, we're here for you. Any questions you have, let us know."

Hart's attention remained on Sam. "I definitely would like a presentation. Sam, would you mind having dinner with me tonight? For business?" His mouth curled in the corner. "Let me look over the packages again and we can talk more about them tonight in my suite." He looked around. "We need privacy."

"Um." Sam stood. "Would you excuse me? I have to go to the bathroom."

Hart winked. "Sure."

Kay got out the booth so Sam could leave. "Are you all right?" she whispered.

"Can you come with me please?" Sam snatched Kay's hand.

Kay got her purse. "Um, we'll be right back, Mr. Baldwin."

He nodded as Sam pulled Kay into the ladies' room.

"What's up with you?" Kay stood by the sink. "Are you all right?"

"Did you see that?" Sam pointed to the door. "How he was acting?"

"A blind person could see it. He was eating out of your hand and it's wonderful!

We got that account for sure."

"No, no, this isn't wonderful." Sam waved her purse. "He wants to sleep with me, Kay."

"So. He's not the first client who wanted to. Just play along to get him to sign the dotted line. No biggie."

"No way I'm having dinner with him." Sam slumped to the sink. "You do it."

"He didn't ask for me, and you gotta do it, Sam. This is a huge deal for us. It could change both of our lives."

She swung around. "I'm not a prostitute, Kay."

"No one's asking you to be! The man asked you to have dinner to discuss the deal, that's all. It's not the first business dinner you've had. I'm sure Mr. Baldwin wouldn't put you in a compromising position."

Sam scoffed. "He looks like he wants to put me in *several* positions."

"I need this to go well. I'm a single mother of two kids, remember? I'm tired of struggling. TriSun is the best job I've had. If we blow this..." Kay sighed, closing her eyes. "Please have dinner with Baldwin. If he comes on too strong, just tell him you're not interested and stick to business."

"Like he'll take no for an answer."

"Hart might be a flirt but he's professional and he's not gonna do anything to jeopardize his reputation. Have dinner with him." Kay poked out her lips. "For me?"

Sam took a deep breath. "Okay."

Kay flung her arms around her. "Thank you."

CHAPTER FOUR

That night, Sam waited in front of room 621, with her briefcase stuffed with pamphlets and documents for her presentation. She just hoped Hart wouldn't give her any trouble and she could do her job and leave.

"Okay." She took a deep breath, knees trembling. She'd reluctantly wore a little spaghetti strapped black dress at Kay's urging.

Sam knocked on the door.

She could handle this. So what if he was the most attractive man she'd ever met? Who cared that his accent made her panties melt? She had to keep her mind on what was important; Kendrick, her future, and Kay's kids. So she'd do the best she could to get TriSun a great deal, but if that meant sex... Hart would be very disappointed.

I think.

He opened the door, looking more scrumptious than a cold glass of lemonade on a hot day. "How are you?" He made even the most innocent questions sound raunchy.

"Fine." Sam exhaled, feeling like she'd pass out. She wanted to get this over with while her loins jumped up and down at the chance to spend more time with him.

He stepped aside. "Come in."

She smiled and passed him to enter. She didn't know what kind of cologne he wore but knew it was expensive because the raspberry scent was so potent she could taste the fruit on her tongue.

"You look lovely." He closed the door, allowing her gaze to fall down his sleek body. He wore a black shirt and black slacks, and the color against his pale skin looked remarkable.

She dropped eye contact for her sanity and looked around the outrageous suite. It was *ridiculous* and so luxurious it made her skin itch. The main room of his suite, which was really three different compartments, looked like it was on an entirely different planet from her and Kay's.

Two floor-to-ceiling windows with blackout curtains boasted a view of the entire beach, and Sam swore she could see all of Bridgetown from his room alone.

Along with elegant additions such as crystal and fine China, he had a bar (yes, a

full-fledged bar), a recreational area with a giant entertainment system, an entire lounge stuffed in the corner and a mini-kitchen.

Wow.

Sam whistled, struggling to take it all in. "So this is what it's like to be rich, huh?"

"The room's okay." He shrugged. "You should see some of the other suites I've stayed in through the years. Would put this one to shame." He stared at her with that same dreamy look he had that morning, and if he wasn't Hart Baldwin, it would've appeared incredibly goofy. "I have a bar way bigger than this one in my NYC home."

"I read you got homes all over the world."

"I have a cottage in Paris, a townhouse in Rome, and estates in Canada, Brazil and

Australia just to name a few."

Her mouth dropped at the absurdity of having so much money. It was one thing to *know* someone was a billionaire but another to hear about the lifestyle.

"Got my own fleet of jets too. Does that impress you?"

She shrugged. "You want it to?"

"Oh, very much I do."

"Must be great to be you. Is there anything you *don't* have?"

"Yes." His face brightened with an impression she could only describe as sinful, and she knew he was talking about *her*. "Hopefully that changes by the time tonight is over."

She cleared her throat, but *nothing* could ease her anxiety at the moment. "Your Wi-Fi getting a good signal? Kay's and mine's been cutting in and out."

"Really?" He raised an eyebrow. "Did you tell the hotel?"

"About three times but I don't think they're taking it seriously."

"Hm." Hart took out his phone and dialed while looking at her. "Yes," he spoke into it. "This is Hart Baldwin."

Sam snickered as she heard the front desk clerk energetically kissing up to Hart over the phone.

"Yes, I'm enjoying my room very much. No... no." Hart sighed, giving Sam that "annoyed" look and she grinned. "I said I'm fine. I have a friend who needs her Wi-Fi looked at. She said she's told you three times, and it's still shite. Can you get on that?" Hart lowered the phone. "What's your room number?"

Sam answered, "Three-oh-nine."

Hart repeated the number to the clerk. "So you'll get on it right now? I thought so. Well, she's not there right now. She's with me but I expect everything to be fine by the time she gets back to her room, understand?"

The hotel clerk nervously rambled off apologies at the top of his lungs.

Hart grimaced, holding the phone away from his face as the man screamed. "Yes, okay. Just get someone on it right now. Thank you, bye." He got off the phone and smirked. "Done."

Sam rocked, holding her grin.

He put his phone up. "Impressed yet?"

She smiled. "Thank you."

"You're welcome."

"So, I thought we were having dinner yet I don't see any."

"It's coming." He glided toward her. "Room service should be here any minute. I like your hair."

She'd folded it into a quick French roll for that messy yet vibrant updo look.

"Thanks." She patted it. "Well, I guess we can get started." She walked across the maroon

carpeting and set her briefcase on the glass table. "Did you look at the packages again?"

"Mm-hmm." His face contorted into that cocky expression guys gave you when they thought you wanted them.

Sam cleared her throat.

Be cool, Sam. He's just a man. You can do this.

She opened the briefcase and glanced over her shoulder to see him coming toward her. "The most popular package is our digital/Internet advertising as I am sure you know."

"Uh-huh." He stopped right behind her, breathing on her neck.

"You'll definitely want to circulate TV spots." She took out her iPad. "I'll show you how we approach that. The best time for Internet advertising is three pm to ten pm."

"I'm aware."

She gave a shaky chuckle. "Yeah, sorry. You've worked with many ad companies." He stood so close she bumped into him whenever she moved.

"You have questions so far?" she asked.

"Yeah. Do you have any panties on?"

She halted. Surely he didn't say what she thought he said. She turned toward him, ready to curse him out when Hart grabbed her head, smothering her with his enormous tongue. She pushed him away, but before she could get the objection out of her mouth, his tongue was in it again, and Hart swirled her around into the dresser.

Everything moved so fast. She couldn't even comprehend what was going on. She knew he wanted her, but this wasn't what she expected. He hadn't even pretended it was about business.

"Mm." Clawing at her dress, he latched his hot lips onto her shoulder and Sam shocked herself when she let out a carnal howl she didn't recognize.

He went from kissing to nibbling and then biting, the pain sending shock waves through her pussy. He felt her up, panting and growling like a bear in heat.

She'd never had sex like this before. So animalistic and raw, no emotion outside of the yearning for each other's bodies. And she liked it. She liked the idea of being fucked with no strings attached and manhandled like a fuck toy at least once in her life.

What the hell is wrong with me?

Hart pushed his large hand under her dress and ripped her panties off in one

swipe. He shoved his hair products off the dresser and hoisted her on top of it, pushing her back against the mirror.

He wasn't saying a word. Just sweating and growling, his eyes drilling into her as he spread her legs and slipped between her thighs.

Hart took a condom from his pocket and ripped the package open with his teeth.

Sam gasped. She wanted to say no. She needed to say no, but she couldn't. Maybe it's because she wanted him unlike she'd wanted any man in a while. Shit, maybe ever. Before Hart, she thought this kind of desire only existed in the movies.

Still not talking, Hart grabbed her face and positioned it to where her eyes were on his and he looked back at her as if to dare her to look away.

Huffing and puffing, he undid his pants and slipped them down to the floor. He grabbed her ass, pushing her pussy against his groin.

Staring right into her eyes, he shoved his cock inside of her and Sam screamed so loudly she thought her throat would split.

"Oh!" It hurt like hell but it was the first time she realized...she liked the pain.

Hart grabbed her thighs and rammed inside her tender hole, stretching her until she felt that burning sensation she hadn't experienced since she lost her virginity.

Moaning and groaning, Hart fucked the shit out of her, banging her so violently that her head repeatedly hit the mirror.

His stare stayed on her. A wild, almost demonic expression on his face.

Sam sucked her lip as the pain of his cock subsided and her pussy relaxed, taking him in deeper.

He slid his hands under her ass, lifting her higher. He pumped fast, and one-by-one, things tumbled until they fell off the dresser.

"Oh!" Hart closed his eyes, his head snapping back and forth. "Ah."

She wondered if this is how British guys did it. She'd read somewhere they were freaks.

She slipped her hands to the front of his shirt and ripped it open, then dragged her fingernails down his chest.

She didn't know why. It was just instinct.

"Yes." Hart pumped. "Scratch me. I like that."

She scratched him again.

"Slower." He panted. "Harder. Until you draw blood."

She gaped.

"*Do* it. Scratch me. I wanna see blood."

She didn't understand it, but she enjoyed hearing him beg. She rarely got to be in control when she and Kendrick fucked, so she'd revel in the chance.

Sam dug her fingernails into his chest as far as she could and brought them down as hard.

"Ah!" He jerked. "Fuck. Shit, that hurt. Woo! Again."

"What?"

"Again." He lifted her legs higher, his dick hitting that spot and urging release.

"Oh." Sam held onto the dresser. "I'm.... I'm coming."

"Scratch me again." He drilled deeper into her. "Scratch me!"

She did it again, and this time she actually felt skin under her nails.

He hollered and Sam was afraid someone might come in, but *he* didn't seem to care.

"Yes." Hart held the dresser for leverage, while he drilled and slammed her into a paradise she never knew existed.

CHAPTER FIVE

Moments later, Sam sat across from Hart on the floor, both lying against the dresser, breathless.

"This can't be the first time you've done this," she said.

"What?" He propped up his knee. "I'm not exactly a virgin if that's what you mean."

"I'm not talking about the sex itself. It can't be the first time you've done *this*." Her stare bounced across the seductive burgundy walls.

"If you're asking if you're the first woman I've wanted so badly that I lost all control, no." He smiled. "You are not. Does it matter?"

She shook her shoulders, pretending she didn't care. "Why should I care?"

"So, did I surprise you?" He wiggled his eyebrows. "Bet you never thought a Brit could fuck like that."

"Why would you say something so ridiculous?"

"You yanks seem to think we're all just stuffy blokes sitting around drinking tea with our pinkies in the air while talking about the queen all day. I fooled *you*, aye?" He snickered. "What about you? I know you're not the type to do this all the time. What is it about me that makes you so wet?"

She scoffed. "You're the one who grabbed *me*."

"You could've said no."

"No... no I couldn't. Before I understood what was going on, you threw me on the dresser and ripped my underwear off."

"So I raped you?"

"No." She slammed her eyes shut. "I'm not saying that."

"So you wanted me?"

She exhaled. "Listen—"

"I listened, Sam. I listened to how loudly you screamed when I fucked you and the deeper I was inside of you, the more you wanted me. Am I wrong?"

"This... we shouldn't have done this. I have a boyfriend."

"I know." He smirked, laying his head against the dresser drawer. "Kay told me."

"What?"

"You know why I'm so good in business, Sam? Because I always investigate anyone who wants to do business with me. I asked Kay about you after you left this morning. She told me you had a guy, and you moved in with him last year."

"What else did she tell you so I can kick her ass."

He grinned. "She told me there's friction between you and your boyfriend. Is she right, Sam? Is there friction in your relationship?"

"No." She lifted her head. "I love him."

"Bullocks." He poked out his lips. "If you loved him you wouldn't be here with me."

"You set me up. Sure is funny I've been here over an hour and dinner hasn't come."

He chuckled. "*You* were dinner."

She knew her ass should've gotten up and left, but she couldn't. He was annoying as hell, but so mesmerizing she couldn't wait to see what else came out of his mouth.

"Why do you care if I have a boyfriend?"

His eyebrows drooped. "I wanted to know about my competition."

"Your competition?" She laughed. "You don't have any competition Hart because there is nothing between us."

"My cock was between us. And you were loving every minute."

"You're disgusting."

"Why? Because I bring out that desire you try so hard to hide under that Miss Goody Two Shoes act? I had your number the moment we met."

"Oh really?"

"Yeah." He wiggled his leg. "You have some fucked up fantasies, don't you, Sam? But you've been afraid to act them out but no more. I'm here now. And I'll teach you how to embrace what you really want. And it sure as hell's not some boring ass guy in Los Angeles, California."

She leaned forward. "Get this straight, Hart. This shit, will never happen again. You are a leech."

He laughed. "A leech?"

"You think I don't know about the way you've shitted all over women? Left them heartbroken with their hearts so battered they never wanna be with a man again?"

He swallowed, his face signaling she'd finally hit a nerve.

"I also know these trysts you have when you go off on business trips aren't new. Bet you've fucked every woman in this hotel."

"Nice try but you can't distract me, Sam. Let's get back to *us*."

"There is no 'us'. You won't do me like you did those other women."

"We're fucking again, Sam. Probably even before you leave this room."

She ignored him. "Are you going to sign with TriSun?"

"Don't know." He licked his lips. "Haven't decided yet."

"We've been working with you for three months. You should have an answer by now."

"It depends."

"On *what*? Let me guess. Me sleeping with you? You can go to hell because that's not gonna happen again—"

"Has your boyfriend ever fucked you, Sam?" His lips curled into a crude smile. "Not made love to you, but fucked? Like I just did? I bet he hasn't because you were so damn thirsty for me."

She scoffed, making a fist.

"You can deny it all you want, but the minute I kissed you, I knew whoever was in your life wasn't shit because he never *fucked* you. I'm talking about bodies slamming together until you can't breathe, bumping and grinding, screams tearing through your throat. Coming in every hole, every which way possible and it feels so damn good that you wouldn't care if the fucking house burned down."

She gasped.

He sat forward, his gaze latched onto her. "I'm talking about sweating, throbbing and clawing. Being so rough you almost tear the skin off each other and even after you've come you still can't get enough."

Her nipples sprouted into daggers.

"I can see your nipples are hard right now." He sat back with that arrogant gleam. "Again, has he ever fucked you, Sam?"

She turned her head away.

"Yeah, that's what I thought."

"You think you know everything and you just met me. Hell, you thought I was a man before you came to the lounge. Yet you know so much."

"I know you want me." He snatched her hand. "This can't end. I'm open for you, Sam, and you feel the same way as me. Fuck logic or your boyfriend. While we're here, we'll have fun. Is that so bad?"

"I..." She stood, fixing her dress. "I gotta go." She walked to the table to get her things.

"I want an affair with you, Samantha." He stood, pushing his hands into his pockets. "I want to drain you dry and see what you're made of."

"You'll ruin me, Hart." She shoved her things into her briefcase. "I can't let you destroy me."

"I wanna give you what you've been missing."

"I gotta go." She rushed past him, but he did what she expected and grabbed her arm. "Have breakfast with me tomorrow."

"What, another invisible meal?" She snatched her arm away and went to the door. "I'll pass."

"I'd like to spend the day with you. Get to know you better and I'll give you my decision on TriSun."

She turned from the door. "I'm not gonna let you use this deal to get close to me."

"I don't have to use it anymore because you're hooked now, Sam." He walked toward her and touched her hair. "And so am *I*."

She scoffed as she left the room.

CHAPTER SIX

Like a fool, Sam met Hart for breakfast the next morning and, like a bigger fool, couldn't wait to see him again. All night she'd thought about them fucking on the dresser and she'd come so many times during the night the sheets were still wet. She hoped the maid didn't think she peed on herself.

This time, they met by the pool, surrounded by others, and actually ate. He verified some things she'd learned about him in the media and he spoke about his father coming over from Britain and how he was already extremely wealthy over there, but America had transformed Baldwin Industries into a business phenomenon.

She talked about life in L.A. and he spoke about what irked him living in NYC.

Sam couldn't remember when she had such an enjoyable conversation with a man. Hart was not only charming, but had a great sense of humor. She loved how he approached things so confidently. When he said arrogant shit, it came from the heart without an ounce of bravado. Unlike most men, he could at least back it up.

Hart ate toast and sucked jam from his fingertip. "It's gotta be driving you crazy to sit so close to me and not touch me. I'm dying over here myself. You keep thinking about last night, don't you?"

She wiggled her shoulders. "No."

He laughed, his slim-fitting T-shirt massaging his small yet athletic pecs. "You're a terrible liar."

"I told you last night can't happen again. Are you gonna sign with TriSun? You said you'd decide."

"I told you to spend the day with me first." He sipped orange juice, winking. "It's just breakfast."

Sam sighed, pursing her lips.

Hart turned in his chair, looking at the tourists who played around in the pool. "Do you like to swim?"

She nodded.

"We can go swimming today."

She looked up as a very handsome man who appeared to be in his mid-to-late twenties hopped out the pool. He swept his wavy black hair back, slinging water down his tan muscles.

Sam squeezed her thighs together, her clit begging to be rubbed. She wasn't only excited because the guy was gorgeous, but he reminded her of sex and all she wanted to do was fuck Hart again whether it was wrong or right.

Hart followed the direction of her gaze. "You like him?"

"Who?" She grimaced as the sexy guy sauntered to a table full of girls, the imprint of his ass and cock showing through his drenched speedos.

"Him," Hart said again. "Come on, Sam. I won't be offended if you find him attractive. I'm sure most women would."

"Are you crazy? I'm not even thinking about that guy and you're no one to be offended. We're not a couple, Hart."

"Do you want to fuck him?"

She balled up her napkin. "Hart, stop it."

"Stop what?"

"Of course I don't wanna fuck him. I don't even know him." She looked over at the stranger, who laughed with the girls. "What's your angle with this?"

"Some men would be jealous if their woman were gawking like you are but we're on a different plane."

"I'm *not* your woman."

"I'm a very unselfish lover, Sam. Maybe to a fault, but I would do anything to satisfy you. Even if it meant letting you be with another man."

"Letting me?" She guffawed. "Hart, I am *not* your girlfriend. I have a boyfriend, remember? And you ain't it."

Hart looked at the guy. "Uh-oh, he's looking at you."

Sam lifted her head, and the sexy guy smiled right at her. And it wasn't just any

smile. He was interested.

"You're so sexy that no man can resist you." Hart pushed the tip of his tongue between his lips. "I want you to have fun, Sam. Just let me know."

"You want to make me happy then drop this asinine conversation." She sipped

orange juice while glancing at the sexy guy. "Your games are tiring already, Hart."

"That's too bad." He winked. "Because you ain't seen *nothing* yet."

HART VOWED TO SHOW Sam the time of her life, and she had no choice but to go along for the ride. Also, she couldn't squander this wonderful opportunity. Who knew if she would ever see this place again, and she certainly wouldn't have the chance to spend it with someone as mesmerizing as Hart. So she threw caution to the wind and vowed to enjoy herself and not worry about what came next.

Unbeknownst to Sam, Hart had scheduled a bus tour ahead of time, as if he just knew she'd agree to spend the day with him. Obviously he'd been right.

They first stopped at Harrison's Cave to see the ancient caverns and become one with nature. They toured the historical Barbados Garrison and took a wild life tour where they fed monkeys and other animals. After lunch, they enjoyed a breathtaking kayak ride.

Though Sam had never seen such amazing sites, the company was what she loved best. Hart was so easy to talk to. She felt like she'd known him all her life, and just being with him was an adventure.

On the tour, they snapped many pictures, including some with them together. As they walked hand in hand and talked about the sights they saw, she felt like his woman. Like a couple, which was more than she could say with Kendrick.

Whenever she looked at Hart, it saddened her how far apart she and Kendrick had drifted, but she loved the feeling Hart gave her. He made her feel alive. Sometimes it was as if Kendrick didn't even remember who she was.

That night, Sam and Hart had dinner in the hotel restaurant then went up to the

third floor. They got to Hart's room, and he took out the keycard. "I got a surprise for

you." He opened the door.

"Well, it'll have to wait until the morning. I'm going to my room. I'm beat."

"You can't go, Sam." He took her hand. "No, no the night's just beginning."

"Hart, please." She slipped her fingers from his grip. "We had a lovely time but this can't go on. I have a boyfriend and I feel like shit doing this behind his back."

"He won't know."

"*I* know. He doesn't deserve this. He's been nothing but loyal to me."

"What do you want out of life, Sam? To be stuck in a loveless relationship, or do you want days and nights full of adventure? You want a man who every time he touches you, you get so hot you don't know if you're coming or going?" He touched her cheek. "Do you want what I can offer you? What I'm giving you?"

"We seem to be off track here." She moved his hand. "I thought you just wanted sex, but I'm not so sure anymore."

"I've never felt this way about a woman." His brows pulled together. "I want all of you. Everything you can offer."

"Hart." She crossed her arms. "What are you saying?"

"You belong with me and before we leave Barbados, I'm gonna make you see it but first, come for your surprise." He widened the door. "Come on, Samantha."

"No." She shook her head. "We can't do this."

"Cheers then." He pointed down the hall. "Stay dead inside. It's obvious that you're more comfortable existing than living."

"You don't think I want to go into that room with you?" She shuddered, squeezing her fingers into fists. "You don't think I want you so badly it hurts? I've never, ever wanted a man as much as I want you but I told you, you'd destroy me. I can't allow that to happen."

"Why would I destroy you?"

"Because I'd be so obsessed with you I wouldn't care how the fuck you treated me and that's dangerous, Hart."

He wrapped his arms around her waist. "You can want me, Sam. It's nothing wrong with that."

"It is wrong." She cursed under her breath. "Just let me go, Hart. Don't make this any harder than it has to be."

"No. All on my mind this entire day was making love to you again and you're not leaving until we do." He pulled her inside and kicked the door closed.

"Hart—"

"Mm." He kissed her, his hands grabbing at her summer dress. "Give in to me, Sam. Give into all those fantasies you've been afraid to experience. It's *right*."

"No." Sam panted, struggling to speak under his kisses.

He stopped. "You want me to stop?"

She shifted her gaze to the table across the room then brought it back to his striking face. "Fuck no." She grabbed his head, pushing her lips over his. "Mm."

The sexy guy from the pool that morning walked from around the corner. He'd tucked his perfect Adonis body into in a snug black T-shirt and dark, slim-fitting jeans.

Sam tore her lips from Hart's. "What the hell?"

"Lorenzo meet Sam." Hart snickered. "Sam, this is Lorenzo. Surely you remember *him*, don't you?"

Also by Stacy-Deanne

Captured

Damaged

Haunted

Possessed

Destined

Stripped Series (Books 1-5)

Stripped Series Books 1-3

Stripped Series (Books 4-6)

Tate Valley Romantic Suspense Series

Now or Never

Now or Never

Chasing Forever

Chasing Forever

Sinner's Paradise

Sinner's Paradise

Last Dance

Last Dance

Tate Valley The Complete Series

The Bruised Series

Bruised

Captivated

Disturbed

Entangled

Twisted

The Good Girls and Bad Boys Series

Who's That Girl?
You Know My Name
Hate the Game

The Studs of Clear Creek County
The White Knight Cowboy
The Forlorn Cowboy
The Lavish Cowboy

Standalone
The Seventh District
Gonna Make You Mine
Empty
Gonna Make You Mine
Protecting Her Lover
What Grows in the Garden
Love is a Crime
On the Way to Heaven
Open Your Heart
Open Your Heart
A Matter of Time
Hero
Outside Woman
The Watchers
Harm a Fly
Harm a Fly
An Unexpected Love
You're the One
Worth the Risk
Dead Weight

Seven's Deadly Sins
Hawaii Christmas Baby
Sometimes Money Ain't Enough
The Best Christmas Ever
Prey
The Good Girls and Bad Boys Series
Bruised Complete Series
Tate Valley Complete Series
The Princess and the Thief
The Little Girl
The Stranger
Oleander
Seducing Her Father's Enemy
Love & Murder: 3-Book Romantic Suspense Starter Set
Paradise
Stalked by the Quarterback
Stripped Complete Series
Tell Me You Love Me
Secrets of the Heart
Five Days
Off the Grid
Sex in Kenya
Fatal Deception
A Cowboy's Debt
Billionaires for Black Girls Set (1-4)
A Savior for Christmas
The Samsville Setup
Trick The Treat
The Cowboy She Left in Wyoming
Theodore's Ring
Wrangle Me, Cowboy
The Billionaire's Slave
The Cowboy's Twin

Also by Venus Ray

Billionaires For Black Girls
Billionaire for the Night
Billionaire Takes the Bride
Billionaire At 36k Feet
Billionaire's Love Trap
Billionaire in the Caribbean
Billionaire Broken
Billionaire Times Two

Sex in the Wild West Series
Maid for Two
Fling on the Frontier
Favor for His Wife
The Carriage Ride
The Bride in the Barn
Sunday Meal

Standalone
Beast
Cindefella

Billionaires for Black Girls Set (1-4)